ON THE BRIGHT SIDE

VENUKA GOYAL

ISBN 979-888521099-7

To my twin boys Atin and Amish

Contents

Acknowledgements

I owe thanks to my father, my sister and my dear friend Namrata for their feedback on the initial drafts of this story.

Note From The Author

A little before midnight on 28th October 2017, I ended up at the hospital in an emergency situation. I've never seen so much blood in my life. Initially the doctor thought I was over-reacting but when the nurse explained my situation to him over the phone he came to the hospital as quickly as he could. "Are you sure you heard two heartbeats?" I kept asking the nurse. "Don't worry," she kept saying, "the doctor is on his way" The last one hour of 28th October 2017 was one of the scariest times of my life.

On the bright side, the first one hour of 29th October 2017 was one of the most memorable times of my life. "I'll send them out to meet their father first," the doctor teased me. "I don't care who they meet first," I said, "I've heard them cry. I know they're okay." Those two cries in the first hour of 29th October 2017 are the two most beautiful sounds in the world to me.

A few days later two birth certificates were issued. Amish Goyal Atin Goyal

'On the bright side' is dedicated to my twin boys Atin and Amish.

1

In the spring of 2009, Varun was sitting in the University health center, his head cradled in his hands, wondering how this happened. What was he going to do? How was he going to get through this? He had moved to the USA to pursue a promising career which would eventually allow him to live a comfortable life with a big house and a nice car. He had moved here for opportunities that would not be as readily available to him in his overpopulated home country. But his situation right now was rather grim. This was not the American dream that he had been chasing. This was a nightmare! As his future seemed more bleak than ever, his mind traveled to his life from one year ago. In the spring of 2008, if someone had told him that he would be in this kind of a situation a year later, he would have laughed at them.

In the spring of 2008, life was simple. The snow had melted and the trees had begun to sprout some green on their branches. Varun had been working with his supervisor Ross as a postdoctoral fellow for about a year or so and had settled comfortably into the work-environment of his lab that was situated on the third floor of one of the buildings that housed the Chemistry Department of the University. His experiments were progressing well and he was hopeful that he would get some well-earned publications soon. Having followed a fairly frugal lifestyle in his eight years in America by always living in apartments and houses on a sharing basis, traveling to India only when it was absolutely essential and spending not more than a dollar on a loaf of bread, Varun had managed to save a bit of money in his bank account. He owned a second hand Toyota Corolla. Well, technically it was fifth hand or something. Having been used by a few faculty members at a University in Michigan and also by a few farmers in the rural area, the car had ended up with one of Varun's housemates when he was a PhD scholar in Michigan. When the housemate got a good job after he graduated, he had practically gifted the car to Varun. Varun had driven the car down to Ohio when he moved here as a postdoc. In the last two years, the car had never really let Varun down. Of course there had been the odd flat tyre to deal with and he had to get the windows fixed once and then the exhaust pipe had come loose in the middle of the highway once; but nothing that couldn't be fixed. By saving up on so many things, Varun had managed to invest some money back home in India even on the modest stipend that he earned during his PhD. Now, as a postdoc, his salary had increased significantly but he more or less continued the lifestyle that he had adopted as a PhD scholar and watched his bank balance grow at a rate faster than before. This bank balance was going to be critical in allowing him to afford finer luxuries of life when he finally got a coveted job as a respectable tenure track faculty member at a University. He would be able to afford a nice house then. He would buy nicer shoes then. Even a large flat screen TV and a Bose surround sound system. But not now. Now was the time to lay the foundations and things were going more or less as planned. All was well in the spring of 2008. The complications started in the summer of 2008, a few weeks after Varun's 31st birthday.

"Last time you got all those shapeless T-shirts and torn jeans!" Varun's mother complained over the phone, "It was so embarrassing! I keep boasting to everyone about how my son is in America and then you come home looking like... like that! You had better go shopping soon. And make sure you click photographs of all your new clothes and send them to me by this weekend. I want to see some nice button-down shirts and actual trousers. Behave like an adult for once!"

"Ho Aai," said Varun, defeated.

Varun's parents had pestered him into planning a visit to India despite his reluctance to do so. His visa status had changed since he started working as a postdoc and he would have to get his visa stamped when he went to India this time. What if there were delays in getting the visa stamped? Ross would absolutely freak out! Regardless, it had been three years since Varun had visited his parents and now his cousin was getting married in India. So his parents had insisted that he visit home. All that was still fine. He would manage somehow. It was the shopping he was dreading at this point. He hated going shopping. And what was the need to buy nice formal clothes when he spent most of his time at the lab anyway? Even Ross wore jeans and a T-shirt to the lab on the days when he didn't have to teach. On the days when he had a lecture, Ross wore button down shirts and trousers. In the winter he would wear a jacket or a sweater to go with it. But Varun wore formal clothes only when he had to make a presentation at a conference. Even when he had been a PhD scholar in Michigan, he had survived almost seven years with only one set of formal clothes that he wore to conferences. He had bought another set for his thesis defense. And now that he was a postdoctoral researcher in Ohio, he hadn't felt the need to buy any more formal clothes at all. But his mother had warned him that the two sets of formal clothes he owned would not be enough on his trip to India this time around. She had given him an ultimatum and now he would have to go shopping!

"We are going to the Mall anyway," Shreya said to Varun in the lab the next day, "we can help you pick out outfits if you're dreading it so much."

Shreya was Varun's labmate, a PhD scholar. She was planning to go shopping with her friend, Anjali.

"Okay," said Varun, "I'll give you guys a ride in my car. It'll save you the trouble of waiting at the bus stop."

It was only at the Mall that the implication of the whole thing struck Varun for the first time. Actually, it was Shreya who pointed it out about 20 minutes into the process of helping Varun pick out some clothes.

"Are you going to be looking at arranged marriage proposals or what?" she asked him casually.

"What?" retorted Varun.

"Why do you seem so shocked?" said Shreya, "You are more than 30 years old and you've never had a girlfriend. I'm sure your parents must be getting ideas."

"No, no," Varun protested, "my cousin is getting married and my mother is worried about how I will make her look in front of the whole extended family. That's why she has been insisting that I buy all these clothes."

But it got Varun thinking. The last time he had visited home about three years ago, his parents had tried to get him to look at arranged marriage proposals.

"But I'm still a student!" Varun had protested back then, "I can't really afford to get married right now. I barely make enough money to support myself."

"I know how much your salary is," his mother had retorted, "I know you earn enough money to pay taxes and I know you earn more money than Sheela Kaki's son who works at an IT company in Pune."

"Aai, he earns in rupees," Varun had explained, "I earn in dollars so it seems like a lot in rupees but the expenses are also more in America."

He had gone on to explain how he lived with roommates and didn't even own a car. How he was busy with his experiments in the lab all the time and didn't have the time to do anything else.

"But a wife will help with things around the house," his mother had explained to him, "You would have someone to take care of you and cook fresh meals for you. There will be many girls who will be willing to move to America and take care of your household for you."

"Ho Aai," Varun had said, "but I didn't get along with half the housemates I had over the past few years. What is the guarantee that I will get along with whoever you choose to get me married to? I know how annoying it can be to live with someone you don't get along with. And with a wife, I won't even be able to just move to a different apartment to sort out the problem!"

Varun had gone on to explain to his family at great length as to why he thought that it would not be a good idea for him to get married and he had absolutely refused to look at proposals for arranged marriage on his last visit to India about three years ago. His parents had not broached the topic with him after that. But once this idea that his parents might be expecting him to look at arranged marriage proposals again this time took seed in his mind, he decided to investigate. He called his younger sister Sonali the next weekend.

"Tell me honestly Sonali," he asked her, "are Aai and Baba looking at arranged marriage proposals for me?"

"No Bhau," she responded, "there is nothing like that. And yeah, when you go shopping next time, make sure you buy a few bottles of perfume for me. I want the nicer and more expensive ones, not the body mist that you got the last time."

"Fine," said Varun, "I'll get perfumes for you. Send me details if there is something specific you have in mind."

"Okay," said Sonali, "I'll send you a message."

Even though Sonali had denied the existence of any plans for getting Varun to look at arranged marriage proposals, Varun feared that his parents might be up to something sneaky. And when he landed in Mumbai the next month, his fears were confirmed. In fact it was much worse than he had feared. His whole family came to Mumbai to pick him up from the airport and instead of booking a taxi for their home in Nasik, they booked one for Pune.

"Pune?" Varun asked his father, confused.

"Her name is Snehalata," his father informed him, "but since it is the same as your mother's name, she has agreed to change it after you both get married."

"Baba!" protested Varun, "How can you spring this on me like this?"

"You are more than 30 years old and you visit India once every 2 or 3 years," his father responded, "what are we supposed to do? Your younger sister also needs to get married at some point!"

"But you could have at least talked to me!" complained Varun.

"And risk you cancelling your trip to India altogether?" his mother interjected.

"Come on Bhau!" Sonali said to him, "I've already met her and she is amazing! And tomorrow is just your engagement, not your wedding!"

"What!" Varun couldn't believe this, "Engagement! So I have no say in this matter then?"

"Of course you do," his mother reassured him, "and so does Hema. She has said that she will give her final consent for getting engaged only after meeting you. So we have not made any elaborate plans."

"Now, who is Hema?" asked Varun.

"Arre Bhau," said Sonali, "Vahini has agreed to change her name to Hema after the wedding. How can there be two Snehalatas in the same home?"

"Vahini!" cried out Varun, getting more shocked by his sister addressing Snehalata as her sister-in-law.

"What else am I supposed to call her?" protested Sonali.

Varun had the urge to just pick up his backpack and make a run for it. He didn't really need the huge suitcase that mostly contained his new clothes and gifts for the family. The important stuff was in the backpack which was lying at his feet. As if reading his mind, his father grabbed him by his elbow and said, "She is a very nice girl and it is not set in stone. You can always say no. In fact even she may change her mind after talking to you. She is too good for you anyway."

And so the family of four got into a cab and drove down to Pune. Varun slept through most of the cab ride and when they reached the hotel that evening and checked in, he was not that tired.

"Do you want to look at her photo?" Sonali asked Varun when they were sitting on a sofa in the small lobby of the three star hotel.

"I don't know," he said, "How does it matter? I'll meet her tomorrow anyway."

"You're so boring!" she complained, "Vahini is so much more fun than you. She agreed at once when I offered to show her your social media pages and your childhood photographs."

"How long has all this been going on anyway?" asked Varun.

"We met her a couple of months ago," said Sonali, "she is Baba's childhood friend's brother's daughter. She is two years younger than you. Apparently you met her when you were kids. I wasn't even born then."

"But why didn't you tell me anything about this before?" asked Varun, "I had even asked you about this specifically when I called that time. And didn't she want to get in touch with me either?"

"Aai and Baba totally forbade everyone from telling you anything," said Sonali, "They thought that you would make some excuses and delay things."

"Fine," Varun relented, "show me her photo."

That night Varun couldn't sleep a blink. Jet lag, of course. But it was also this weird feeling of anticipation. Not only had he seen Snehalata's photograph, he had sent her a friend request on social media which she had promptly accepted. Her social media account was flooded with smiling photographs of her at what looked like picnics and vacations with family and friends. She seemed to be about average in height and had a narrow build. She seemed to prefer securing her hair with a broad clip at the back of her head and she seemed to prefer wearing jeans and kurtas on casual outings. Even though the idea of getting married was scary, Snehalata didn't seem to be so scary after all. There was something endearing about her mousy little face and based on her profile she liked traveling, cooking, reading novels and watching movies. That seemed pretty normal.

'I'm so glad that I'm finally allowed to contact you,' was the first message she sent him.

'Hi,' Varun responded to her message.

'I'm looking forward to meeting you tomorrow,' she retorted.

'Same here'

'Do you like shrikhand?'

'Yes'

'I'm making shrikhand for dessert tomorrow.'

'Ok'

'Elaichi flavour?'

'Sounds good'

She was making shrikhand for him for lunch and he hadn't even known about her existence till a few hours back. This was so surreal.

'You must be tired from your long journey,' she messaged him, 'You should probably go to sleep now.'

'I can't. Jet lag.'

'Oh! How does it feel?'

'Jet lag?'

'I've never travelled outside India. Never experienced jet lag.'

Varun found himself chatting with Snehalata for a couple of hours discussing everything from jet lag to eating store-bought tortillas instead of home-made rotis. She told him about her love for travelling and her interest in cooking.

'Do you like to travel?' she asked him at some point of time.

Varun wasn't all that into travelling but he didn't mind it either. He didn't quite know how to respond to her question.

'I went to Cedar Point with my labmates last year. It was fun,' he replied eventually.

'Cedar Point?' she asked him.

'It's an amusement park close to where I live. It has good roller coasters.'

'Wow! I love roller coasters.'

That came as a bit of a surprise to Varun. Did that mousy little woman really love roller coasters?

'I also like roller coasters,' he informed her.

'I went to EsselWorld in Mumbai when I was in school. It was so much fun!'

'Cedar Point is even better than that'

'I hope I can go there sometime'

'My sister told me that we met each other when we were kids'

'It seems we met at a wedding function. I'll send you a photograph.'

Soon Varun saw a group photograph from a wedding. Women draped in silk sarees and loaded with glittering gold jewellery. Men dressed in formal shirts and pants.

'Are you the little toddler in the pink frilly dress?'

'Yes. And you're the kid in the blue shirt, right?'

'Yes'

Chatting with Snehalata made Varun feel slightly less weird about the next day but he still couldn't believe that he was expected to get engaged to her after meeting her just once.

∞∞∞∞

"Bhau!" Sonali yelled at Varun, "You have to wake up now or we'll get late!"

Varun had dozed off early in the morning and now he was being badgered by his family to get ready quickly as they were supposed to go to Snehalata's home for lunch. He

10

dragged himself out of bed and took a shower. And as he took the shower he thought about the task at hand. What was he going to do this afternoon? Was he going to stand his ground and firmly reject the marriage proposal? Or was he going to give in to his family's sneaky scheme? The thing is, even if he rejected this proposal, he was going to be in India for the next few weeks. And in these few weeks he would be attending his cousin's wedding. That would be a very fertile ground for letting his parents' imagination run wild. They would probably try to get him to look at every single girl at the wedding and create really uncomfortable situations for him. And all said and done, Snehalata didn't seem to be so bad after all. They seemed to have a few things in common and chatting with her the previous night had actually been pretty okay. The fact that they had met with each other as kids almost seemed like fate. He would make up his mind after meeting her, but maybe he would meet her with an open mind, he decided. Maybe he would not be totally hell bent on rejecting this marriage proposal.

Varun soon stepped out of the shower and found that his sister had already selected an outfit for him to wear. It was a pinstriped shirt and black trousers that he had bought at the Mall about a month ago. But as Varun was getting dressed he was hit by a sudden pang of guilt. He had brought gifts for everyone from America but he hadn't got one for Snehalata. Of course, he hadn't known about her existence when he had gone shopping the previous week, but still, he wished that when he met her for the first time, it wouldn't be empty handed. But then again, would it be appropriate for him to take a gift for her? What if he decided to not go ahead with the engagement after meeting her? And what if she rejected him after talking to him, like Baba had said the previous day?

"Where are the perfumes I had asked you to bring?" Sonali asked Varun as he got ready to leave.

"In my suitcase, where else?" he retorted.

"I have some wrapping paper," said Sonali.

"What are you talking about?" asked Varun.

"It's okay," said Sonali, "if you don't like Vahini and are planning to reject this proposal then it's better if you don't give her a gift."

"No!" said Varun, "Give me the wrapping paper. What are you going to do with so many perfumes? I'll give one to Snehalata."

"Her friends call her Sneha," said Sonali.

"Yeah, Sneha," said Varun, getting rather red in his face, "I'll give one to Sneha."

"You're welcome," said Sonali as she handed him a wrapping paper with a cheeky smile on her face.

Sneha was nervous. She had already rejected multiple marriage proposals in the past couple of years and her parents were getting impatient. Her father was going to retire from his job soon and even though Sneha had a job and was in principle independent and settled in her life, she knew that her father would not rest easy until he saw Sneha, his youngest child, married into a respectable family.

"Please get married soon and let your father retire in peace," her mother had pleaded with her on multiple occasions.

Sneha didn't want to cause her parents any grief but somehow she had not been able to say yes to any of the men who had been paraded in front of her.

"Varun's father is well known to our family and the boy is well educated," Sneha's father had announced one day, a few months ago, "In fact, he has a PhD from abroad. He is a scholar and a respectable person. What more could we ask for?"

"But Baba," Sneha had protested, "how can I move so far away from home? And what will I do there? Will I be able to get a job in America?"

"Don't be silly," her mother had interjected, "taking care of a house and a family is also a lot of work and responsibility. At your age, you shouldn't delay having kids either."

"Aai!" Sneha had protested, "I'm not even married yet and you're talking about kids!"

"Just look at his photograph and meet his family next weekend," her mother had said, "they are going to be in Pune for a family function anyway and they want to meet you."

Even though Sneha had been reluctant at first, after seeing Varun's photograph where he was dressed up smartly in navy blue trousers and blazer, she had suddenly become less averse to the idea of getting married. His metal frame glasses with thick lenses, his hair that sat on his head in wildly undulating waves, even the hint of a paunch that peeked out from the navy blue blazer he was wearing. All of it was not so bad after all. And the next week, when she met Varun's bubbly sister who showed Sneha more of his photographs, Sneha couldn't help but notice how attractive his smile was.

"Bhau is not much of a singer," Sonali confided in Sneha, "but he likes listening to music. And he likes watching movies too."

The more Sneha found out about Varun, the less averse she became to the idea of getting married to him.

Sneha had known for the past couple of months that she would be meeting Varun on this day. But when the day actually arrived, she found herself utterly unprepared. She wasn't sure whether the fact that they had chatted with each other for a couple of hours the previous night was making her less nervous or more nervous. She had only photographs of Varun for reference till the previous evening but now she also had a chat for a reference. She knew now that he liked shrikhand and hoped that he would like the one that she had made for lunch that day. She adjusted the pallu of the pink silk saree her mother had helped her wear and wondered if the half a dozen safety pins would indeed succeed in keeping the ensemble in place. Her mother had been pushing her to wear more jewellery but she had settled for a small gold necklace, matching gold jhumkas and half a dozen pink bangles on each wrist. "They're here!" her mother announced and Sneha hurriedly put a small red bindi on her forehead, in between her eyebrows, and checked her hair for flyaways one last time. She rushed out of her bedroom but then checked herself. She shouldn't appear to be too impatient, she told herself. She walked down the tiny corridor of the small two-bedroom flat where she lived with her parents and reached the hall. Sneha walked past the dining table and stood behind a sofa in the sitting area. Her elder sister Hetal was standing at the main door of the flat, greeting who she hoped would be Sneha's future in-laws. Hetal's husband had an important meeting at the office that day and had excused himself from the event and Hetal's little daughter was with Hetal's in-laws who lived in the same city.

"What about the other necklace that I had given you?" Sneha's mother hissed at her.

"Aai!" she hissed back, "Trust me, I know what I'm doing!"

Soon both families greeted each other and the elders sat at the six seater dining table for lunch. It was decided that the youngsters would eat later.

"Sonali," said Hetal, "will you please come and help me with something in the kitchen?"

Sonali promptly got up from the sofa, gave a knowing smile to Sneha, and walked off with Hetal. Even though they were in plain view of their families, Sneha and Varun were now in a position to have a private chat with each other. Sneha shifted a little in the single-seater sofa she was sitting in. Somehow, despite having taken the lead in chatting with Varun via text messages the previous night, Sneha found herself not quite up to initiating a conversation with him at this point. Varun was sitting in the middle of a three seater sofa that was kept perpendicular to the small sofa that Sneha was sitting on. He got up and took a step towards Sneha. Then he sat down on the edge of the sofa that was closest to Sneha, his knees inches away from hers.

"I have a gift for you," said Varun and held out a small box covered with wrapping paper.

Sneha looked at him, surprised.

"You didn't have to," she said.

"I wanted to," he said.

Sneha accepted the small box with a smile and asked him, "How was your exam? Did you do well?"

"Exam?" asked Varun.

By the look on his face, Sneha realized that he had no idea what she was talking about.

"I... I was told not to contact you the past couple of months," she explained to him, "I was told that you had an important exam and we shouldn't disturb you. There was no exam, was there?"

"I... yes... of course! That exam!"

"You're not a good liar."

"Yeah, a lot of people have said that to me."

"So tell me the truth."

"Last time I visited home, my parents tried to get me to look at marriage proposals but I didn't listen to them. I think that's why they decided to keep me in the dark and spring this on me when I landed here yesterday."

"So... you didn't know about me at all till yesterday?"

"No"

"And you don't want to get married, do you?"

"I... I don't know. To be honest, the idea of getting married is a bit scary."

"Yeah, it's scary for me too. I'll have to leave my home and my family. And if I get married to you then I'll have to leave my job too and go to a foreign country where I would know no one. And your mother would want me to change my name."

Varun looked at Sneha as she listed reasons why marrying Varun would not be a good idea for her and he was beginning to regret giving her the gift. Maybe she was going to decide against getting engaged to him. Sonali would have liked this perfume. It was the most expensive one out of all the ones he had bought.

"On the bright side," said Sneha at some point, a faint smile on her lips, "if I get married to you, I will be able to travel so far away from home for the first time in my life. It's scary but also exciting. Like being on a roller coaster."

"We could visit Cedar Point sometime," Varun suggested, "and we could also drive down to Niagara Falls. It's only five hours from where I live."

"Wow!" said Sneha, her eyes glittering with excitement, "Isn't that the largest waterfall in the world? When I read about it in a textbook in school I wondered what it would be like to actually see it."

Varun had never wondered what it would be like. Some of his labmates had gone to Niagara Falls over a weekend the previous month but Varun had chosen to stay back and get some experiments done in the lab. But when he saw how the expression on Sneha's face brightened upon the thought of going there, he found himself planning the logistics.

"I have enough money saved up to buy a new car," said Varun, "maybe we could go on a few road trips in the spring. It won't be a good idea to drive too much in the winter... with the snow and all."

"Does it snow a lot where you live?"

"Yeah. And when the temperature approaches -20 degrees, we keep our fingers crossed that none of the pipes will burst. The building where my lab is located is really old."

"That sounds kind of scary."

"Don't worry, there is central heating in all the buildings. And I can afford to rent a one bedroom apartment in one of the residential areas close to campus. Columbus is not a very expensive city to live in."

Varun found himself trying to convince Sneha about how moving to America was not that scary after all.

"And you don't really have to change your name," he found himself saying, "I live so far away from my parents. How does it matter if your name is the same as my mother's name? No one calls her Sneha anyway. Even my father calls her Lata."

"It's okay," said Sneha, "I don't mind if I go by Hema when we visit your parents."

And that afternoon, with the blessings of their parents, Sneha and Varun got engaged.

The next few weeks that Varun spent in India were really hectic. Between getting his visa stamped, for which he had to go all the way back to Mumbai, attending his cousin's wedding, for which he travelled with his whole family to Aurangabad, and catching up with friends in Nasik, Varun couldn't really find time to meet Sneha again. What's more, he had brought his work home. He was working on writing a paper based on some of the experimental results he had got. Sneha too was busy with her full-time job. They called each other once in a while and were relieved that no red flags popped up during their conversations but even as Varun got ready to fly back to America, Sneha and Varun were far from being emotionally attached to each other.

3

A few weeks after his engagement, Varun was back in Ohio, having a rather uncomfortable conversation with Ross.

"I know that I just took a few weeks off to visit India," Varun found himself explaining to Ross, "but I will need two weeks off again after a couple of months."

"We really need to get the experiments in the project going, Varun," Ross warned him, "I'm going to have to write a few grant proposals soon and I need more preliminary results. I can't have the lab run out of funds and I'm counting on you to get this done."

"I know," said Varun, "I'll make sure I get the experiments done even if it means working on weekends, but I will have to take those two weeks off in the fall. I'm getting married. I have to be there."

"Oh!" said Ross, "Congratulations!"

And eventually, Varun's leave was sanctioned.

There was a ton of work to get done in the lab the next couple of months. With the hectic schedule and the time difference, Varun was not really able to find much time to chat with Sneha. They video called a couple of times but it was too much trouble really. She hadn't quit her job yet and she was also very busy with preparations for the wedding. Juggling their schedules to find time to talk to each other was not turning out to be possible very often. And when

Varun flew back to India for his wedding, it still felt like he was getting married to a stranger.

Sonali had chosen a moss green silk kurta for her Bhau to wear at the wedding and Varun felt quite self-conscious wearing it as it had quite a bit of golden zari detailing on it.

"Oh! Don't be silly," Varun's mother said to him on the morning of the wedding, "a groom from America has to wear an impressive kurta. Your sister has picked a perfect outfit for you."

"I don't know about the America part," Sonali interjected, "but I know how beautiful Vahini is going to look in her saree and I didn't want my Bhau to look like a stupid monkey in front of her!"

Varun glared at her and Sonali vanished from the room after showing him a good portion of her tongue.

The wedding ceremony was traditional yet simple. Sneha was wearing a bottle-green silk saree with a broad red border and golden zari detailing. The customary green glass bangles tinkled at her wrists and the customary nose ring decorated with white beads made her look every bit the traditional bride. A morning muhurat was chosen and certain government officials were invited to the wedding to speed up the process of getting the marriage certificate made. At the lunch reception after the wedding certain documents were signed and the paperwork for Sneha's US visa application was completed.

The next week was quite awkward for Sneha. She drove down to Nasik with Varun and his family and they had a reception party the next evening that was attended by extended family and close friends. Sneha had practiced draping a saree many times by now but she needed some help with getting things perfect. But everyone was so busy with the festivities that she didn't know who to ask for help.

She was old enough that people probably expected her to know how to do this anyway. She somehow managed on her own and was relieved when she made it through the reception without any disasters. Varun's parents' house had only two bedrooms and Sneha felt bad for Sonali as she volunteered to give up her bedroom for Varun and Sneha and proceeded to sleep on the narrow day-bed in the living room at night. Even in the bedroom, Varun treated Sneha like a roommate he barely got along with.

Two days before Varun was to fly back to America, Varun's mother suggested to him in the evening, "Why don't you take Hema to a restaurant for dinner tonight?"

Varun looked at his mother who was sitting at the dining table, munching some chivda. Then he looked at Sneha who was in the kitchen making tea for everyone, looking rather somber. She was decked up in gold jewellery that his mother had insisted she wear and she was wearing an embroidered salwar-kameez, looking like a new bride. And soon her husband was going to fly abroad, leaving her behind to make tea for her in-laws every evening. Why had a successful working professional like her agreed to something stupid like this? He hadn't really seen her smile the last few days apart from the fake smiles at the reception and when some guests were visiting. He felt sorry for her.

"Okay," Varun said to his mother and walked into the kitchen. He stood next to Sneha as she got the pot of boiling tea off the gas stove and started to strain it into small white teacups.

"Will you go out for dinner with me?" he asked her, "There is this restaurant close by that serves pretty good kadhai paneer."

Sneha gave a little nod and proceeded to keep the teacups on a green plastic tray. Then she turned towards him with the green tray in her hands. She moved the tray a bit towards him and Varun picked up one of the white teacups. Then Sneha proceeded to walk out of the kitchen and serve tea to the rest of the family.

Later that evening, on their first dinner date, Varun asked Sneha, "Are you missing your family?" She gave him a nod and proceeded to stare at her hands that lay clasped on the brown table.

"You should go and stay with them once I go back to America," he suggested.

"Your parents won't be too happy if I did that," she said, "a new bride is supposed to live with her in-laws, not with her parents." Then she looked at Varun, gave him a half-hearted smile, and said, "On the bright side, Sonali is a really nice girl. I like spending time with her. Once you are gone, she will be my roommate. It'll be fun."

"Would you prefer Sonali as a roommate over me?" Varun asked her.

"We are supposed to be a married couple, not just roommates," said Sneha.

Varun looked at the menu and asked her, "Will you have tandoori roti with the kadhai paneer?"

"Do you like naan?"

"I don't mind naan."

"Will you share one with me? I like naan but it is too big for me to finish. I eat it only when I find someone to share it with."

"Okay," said Varun and they ended up having kadhai paneer and naan for dinner.

∞∞∞∞

"I'll book a flight for you the moment you have your visa," Varun promised Sneha at Mumbai airport a week after the wedding.

Sneha was staring at her toes. She was wearing a pink kurta with jeans. She gave him a nod but didn't say anything. Varun didn't really know what to do. Was he just supposed to leave her by herself, standing there like that? As if reading Varun's mind, Sneha looked up at him. She gave him a forced smile. Then she glanced back at Varun's family that was standing several feet away, his mother barely managing to control her tears. Then Sneha looked at Varun again, gave him a quick peck on his cheek, turned around and walked back to his family. Soon Varun was waving goodbye to Aai, Baba, Sonali and Sneha.

∞∞∞∞

By the time Sneha landed at Newark airport it was late fall and the winds had begun to get chilly. After clearing customs she was directed to an area where her baggage would be checked-in for her connecting flight.

"Chalo, chalo!" a rather tall and intimidating looking African American man announced as she approached the conveyor belt where she was supposed to drop off her large suitcases.

Those familiar Hindi words announced in an unfamiliar American accent made her feel a bit strange in this country that smelled like an expensive brand of soap or maybe a room freshener. Sneha wasn't sure. She wasn't sure what this smell was and she wasn't sure if those words that came as rather unexpected to her given her location made her feel more at home or more homesick.

At a security check where her cabin baggage was examined, Sneha was asked to step aside from the queue.

"There is a strange smell in your bag that I'm concerned about," the security personnel announced, "can you tell me what it is? It seems to be some sort of chemical."

Sneha looked at the bag that her father, who was a Chemical Engineer, had got in one of his official meetings. It had the word 'chemical' written on it in one corner along with certain other technical terms. The bag had been sitting in a closet for several months before Sneha had cleaned it out and used it.

"Naphthalene balls," Sneha explained.

"Is that some chemical?" the security personnel inquired.

Just then another security personnel came over and grabbed Sneha's bag. He took a sniff and gave it back to her.

"It's moth balls," he explained to his colleague.

Sneha was let through the security and it was only when she sat herself down on a blue chair at the gate where she would board her connecting flight that she took out her American phone from her bag and switched it on.

"There won't really be any pay phones that you would be able to use at Columbus airport," Varun had said to her when he had handed the phone to her at Mumbai airport before he left for America, "Switch this on when you are in America. I have added this to my family plan."

Sneha took a deep breath and then she made her first phone call in America.

"Hello," Varun's voice greeted her.

"Hi! I'm at Newark airport."

"I was waiting for your call. I hope they didn't bother you at customs and immigration."

"No. It was fine. I'm at the boarding gate."

"Did you eat something? You won't get anything to eat on the local connecting flight. They will just give you some juice."

"I don't feel like eating anything."

"Do you have something with you to munch on?"

"I kept those granola bars that you had given me. I have a few left."

"Okay. You should be fine then."

"I need to go to the bathroom. I'll call you when I board the flight."

"Okay"

"See you soon"

Sneha cut the call and started sobbing uncontrollably. What kind of hell was she in? She couldn't bear the thought of not being able to see her family again for god knows how long.

∞∞∞

By the time Varun reached Columbus airport and parked his car, he had begun to experience some of the reasons why he had been scared at the idea of getting married. He had already spent so much money and there would be more expenses to take care of. Over the past few weeks he had moved out of his rather economical accommodation that he shared with multiple housemates and moved into a one bedroom apartment not too far away from the University. He had upgraded his car to a new Toyota Yaris. It was smaller than his older car but so much more comfortable and reliable. It was a car in which he would be able to take Sneha on the road trips he had talked to her about. But could he really afford those road trips? Did he have the time? Would it be worth the expense? Varun wasn't sure.

4

It was the spring of 2009 and Sneha was sitting on a bench in the University health center. She glanced at Varun who was sitting beside her, his head cradled in his hands. What was she going to do? How was she going to get through this? Terminating the pregnancy was not really an option. She had heard too many stories about things going wrong with that. Would she have to go back to India? Would her parents support her? As her future seemed more bleak than ever, Sneha's mind went back to her first day in this strange country.

When she had landed at Columbus airport in the fall, she had never imagined things would end up like this. In the fall of 2008, Sneha was waiting for her suitcases at the conveyor belt at the airport in Columbus. Her eyes wandered away from the conveyer belt and she spotted Varun walking towards her. She waved at him and he waved back at her. Soon he came and stood beside her. Sneha took a deep breath. She did like travelling but she had never traveled alone before. It had always been with family or friends. Sneha had been so stressed out in the last 24 hours, constantly worried about losing something from her luggage, feeling uncomfortable about not being able to understand English, a language she had learnt since she was a child, because of the unfamiliar accent and not being able to find food that seemed appetizing enough. She tried to imagine what it must have been like for Varun when he came so far away from home for the first time. He would not have had anyone to warn him about not getting food on the domestic flight. He would not have had anyone give him a phone that he could switch on when he reached America.

"Is that your suitcase?" Varun suddenly asked Sneha.

She looked at the conveyor belt.

"Yes," she said, "it's the blue one with the pink ribbon tied to the handle."

"See," said Varun, "it was so easy to spot it with the ribbon."

Sneha looked at Varun as he proceeded to grab the huge suitcase from the conveyor belt. He was the reason behind her miserable journey but at least he had made her journey as easy as he could.

∞∞∞∞

Sneha had already seen Varun's apartment on a video call before but actually walking into the space felt surreal. The apartment felt smaller, somehow, and the bare walls and windows without any drapes made it feel sterile. The kitchen was tiny. Was there really any storage space in there? The bedroom was a decent size but it felt so bare and so cold. Had she really left her family, her home, her life, her everything for this? Then she looked at Varun as he went about setting up the dining table. Even though the dining table was just a small square folding table with folding chairs, there was dal and rice on it. It was the most appetizing looking meal she had come across in the last 24 hours. Varun had cooked for Sneha that evening. That was way more than what her own father had ever done for her mother. On the bright side, Sneha said to herself, she had Varun.

The next few weeks were rather strange for Sneha.

"We have to share the washer and dryer with the other tenants of the building," Varun explained to her the day after she arrived, "The laundry room is in the basement. Come I'll show you how to use it."

This made Sneha feel rather uncomfortable. How was she supposed to share a washing machine with complete strangers? She won't know what they had been washing in it before. But she didn't complain and accepted whatever came her way. And there were indeed more surprises in store for her.

"They call it okra here," said Varun pointing to a box of ladies fingers in the supermarket next weekend. Then he pointed to the brinjal and said, "and these are supposed to be eggplants."

When Sneha started to look at some fresh tomatoes, Varun warned her, "Those are very expensive. Especially the tomatoes on the vine. We can buy a few of them for salad and stuff but for cooking gravies the canned tomatoes turn out much cheaper."

Sneha had never had to worry about the cost of fresh vegetables before. And were the canned tomatoes really going to taste as good in the gravies? She wasn't sure. She had already realized that the salt here in America was less salty and the sugar less sweet than the one she had in India.

"On the bright side," Sneha said, forcing a smile on her lips, "I won't have to chop tomatoes."

All of it was not so depressing though. They also went shopping for furniture and furnishings for the apartment.

"It's called DIY furniture," Varun explained, "we will have to assemble it ourselves but it turns out so much cheaper."

"This sounds like fun," Sneha played along, "I've never assembled a bookshelf before."

With a new bookshelf, bright shower curtains, new drapes on the windows, a new set of bedding and a few bright doormats, Sneha felt the apartment looked a lot less bare. They even bought some more plates and China mugs and slowly Varun's apartment started looking like Sneha and Varun's home.

Getting married was not so bad after all, Varun found out after some time. He no longer had to cook, clean or do his laundry.

"This is the least I can do," Sneha had insisted, "I can't even get a job here on this visa status. What else am I going to do all day? I can read only so many books and watch only so many movies."

At some point of time, she even got used to driving on the right side of the road and got into the habit of dropping Varun off at the University in the morning a couple of times a week before taking the car with her on a grocery run.

"Don't worry," she said to him on the first day she executed this plan, "I know to buy canned tomatoes and I'll pick up a gallon of milk if the half-gallon of milk is not available at a discount."

With his workload on the home front having practically vanished, Varun had managed to become even more efficient at work. Also, with Sneha taking charge of the kitchen, Varun's lunch boxes that he took to the Department had become more elaborate.

"Wow!" commented Shreya at lunch time one day, "That looks like a feast! I don't remember the last time I bothered to cook both rice and roti for a meal!"

"Sneha enjoys cooking," Varun retorted, "and she insists on doing this every morning."

"Lucky you," said Shreya with a smile, "when are you calling us home to meet Sneha?"

And on a weekend that winter, half a dozen Indian PhD scholars and postdocs from the University landed up at Varun's apartment at lunch time. They raved about Sneha's cooking and polished off all the vessels down to the last bowl of shrikhand.

"That's the best meal I've had in a while," commented Shreya, "Thank you so much Sneha."

"You're most welcome," said Sneha, "you should come over again sometime."

That evening, even after all the guests had left, Sneha was in a good mood. Maybe it was because she had met so many new people that day. That too Indians who she could relate to and connect with over food, music, movies and cricket. As she was bustling about the apartment, clearing up the remnants of the lunch party, Varun suggested to her, "Maybe we should go out for dinner tonight. You've already spent so much time cooking today. It doesn't make sense for you to cook dinner too."

"Okay," said Sneha and they drove down to Chipotle, a Mexican restaurant, later in the evening.

"I can't believe how early the sun sets these days," Sneha said as they settled into their seats with a brown rectangular table between them.

Sneha looked a bit different now than when they had first met, Varun noticed. She had gained the slightest bit of weight and her face seemed to glow for some reason. Her wardrobe had changed significantly with the progressing winter and she looked really smart in the brown jacket that they had bought for her at a discount from JC Penny the previous weekend.

"Sometimes I barely get to see the sun in the winters," said Varun, "It's already dark outside by the time I leave the lab. The winters can be really gloomy. I think that's why the people here have their main festivals in the winter. They light up the lawns and the common areas to celebrate Christmas and the New Year. I got so sick of Christmas carols the first winter I was in America. They were all over the radio and the TV and in the Mall. But I think these festivities in the winters lighten up the gloom a bit. I've grown to like the Christmas cheer now."

"How did you live all alone for so many years?" asked Sneha, "I can't imagine how I would have survived here if you weren't around."

"I came here a long time ago," said Varun, "I was a student back then. There was an Indian Student Association at my University in Michigan that helped me settle in. And then there was so much coursework and lab work and things to keep me busy. I made some friends along the way. Time flies, I guess. Sometimes I can't believe I've lived in this country for so long."

"Is this burrito actually meant for one person?" asked Sneha as she peered into the shallow basket set on the table in front of her.

"That's exactly what I felt like when I first came to America," said Varun with a smile, "I could never finish a portion size. I always had to box half my food when I left a restaurant."

"I guess I'm lucky to have you to share the food with," said Sneha, "I don't like the idea of taking leftover food from the restaurant back home."

That night when they were in bed, Varun pulled Sneha closer to him. She smiled at him and pecked him on his lips. It wasn't the first time they did it, but somehow, it felt different that night. Less awkward, more intimate. And as the winter progressed and the nights got longer, they got more comfortable with each other. In fact, Sneha got a lot more comfortable than Varun had ever imagined.

"Let's do it in the bathtub tonight," she suggested one night after dinner.

Varun almost dropped the plate that he was washing.

"Are you serious?" he asked her after a while.

"Well..." she said, a suggestive smile on her face.

"You do know that our bathroom is not that fancy," he said.

"I cleaned it out real nice today," she said, "and we can switch off the lights and light the scented candles we got from Bath and Body Works."

"I'm not so sure about this," said Varun.

"Let's give it a shot," insisted Sneha, "what's the worst that can happen?"

Later, when they slipped and fell on top of each other in the bathtub, Sneha let out a shriek and started giggling uncontrollably.

"On the bright side," she said, "we don't seem to have broken any bones."

Varun smiled at her and said, "If we had ended up with broken bones, I guess, the bright side would have been that we have a good health insurance plan."

"See," said Sneha, "you're getting a hang of this now."

They never tried doing it in the bathtub again.

As the winter months progressed, Varun's work at the lab became more manageable. He didn't have to work on weekends any more. At some point of time he realized that he could, after all, afford to take a couple of days off here and there. Maybe he could take Sneha on a couple of road trips that she would like.

"Of course we will go to Niagara Falls," said Varun at the dinner table one night, "but didn't you also want to go to Cedar Point? I think we should do that first."

"Yes, of course," said Sneha, "I don't want to miss the roller coasters."

"I think we should buy a nice GPS," said Varun, "it will come in handy on all the road trips."

They bought the GPS and got the car serviced and they were really looking forward to the road trips they had planned. But as luck would have it, a few days before they were supposed to go to Cedar Point, Varun came home to a distraught Sneha.

"What's wrong?" he asked her when he realized that she hadn't greeted him in her usual manner and was sitting really still on the sofa. When he walked over to her and sat down beside her, tears started streaming down her face.

"We can't go to Cedar Point this weekend," she said, "I'm pregnant."

Varun couldn't believe what she was saying.

"How is this possible?" he blurted, "Are you sure?"

"I didn't realize for some time because my period has been a bit irregular," said Sneha, "but the home pregnancy test turned out positive today."

6

It was the spring of 2009 and Varun was sitting in the University health center, his head cradled in his hands, wondering how this happened. What was he going to do? The sonography reports had confirmed the pregnancy and Varun couldn't believe what was going on.

"Let's go," Sneha finally said to him, "I need to cook dinner. We'll get late."

Varun slowly got up from the bench and started walking towards the exit. Sneha followed him and they made their way to the car.

"You got the parking validated, didn't you?" Sneha asked Varun.

"Yeah," he said as he got into the car.

Sneha got into the front passenger seat and secured her seatbelt.

"Do twins run in your family?" Varun asked her.

There was no history of twins in Varun's family and this had come as a complete shock to him. To be honest, Varun didn't really think he was ready to be a father quite yet. There was too much going on work-wise. He had a career to think about. He would have preferred to wait for some time to have kids. He would have preferred to wait till he got a proper job and had a house of his own. And they had been careful. But apparently birth control had some rate of failure and it had failed so royally in their case that now they were going to have twins! He had somehow managed to put up a brave front when they had found out about the pregnancy a few weeks ago. But how were they going to manage twins? Two car seats, double the number of clothes, double the number of diapers. How were they going to afford all this? And what about the sleepless nights that came with babies? How would he finish up his publications and apply for jobs with all this drama going on at the home front? Was he going to end up being a postdoc forever? Would Ross have funds to let Varun continue working in his lab much longer? Would he have to forget about faculty positions and just apply for another postdoc and risk being stuck as a serial postdoctoral researcher who never quite rose on the academic ladder? What kind of a nightmare was this? When would he ever be able to afford the Bose surround sound system? He could see only diapers in his near future! Getting married had turned out to be fine as he ended up getting along with Sneha and they shared responsibilities with each other. But babies would be so needy! They would not share any responsibilities! And with twins it would be double the headache and double the expense!

Sneha looked at Varun and said, "There are a few twins on my mother's side of the family."

She was really freaking out right now. Could they really afford the expense? And were they ready to have babies at this point? They had known each other only for a few months and there was so much they wanted to do before settling into a family life. There was this whole continent that Sneha had been looking forward to exploring! The only way all that would happen at this point would be by terminating the pregnancy. But Sneha was not that young after all. She would be 30 years old soon. And she had heard about too many bad things happening with terminating pregnancies. Even though she wasn't quite ready for it now, having kids was always part of the plan in the long run. What if she had trouble getting pregnant later on in life? She would certainly curse herself for terminating this pregnancy then. And would she really have the heart to get rid of those two little hearts that were beating so furiously inside of her? She didn't think so. Terminating the pregnancy didn't seem like such a good idea. But what would she do? Wouldn't it be cheaper to give birth to the babies in India? Wouldn't her family be available to help her out with things back home? But if she went to India would her family support her decision to stay away from her husband for a few years? And would she actually be able to live with her parents? Or would she be forced to live with her in-laws? That would not be a very good option for her. She would have to convince her parents to support her and take her to Pune directly from Mumbai Airport. As she was reeling with the implications of the whole thing, words started tumbling out of Sneha's mouth, "Most of the women on my mother's side of the family are so much taller. I have got this short height and small frame from my father's side of the family. I look like a dwarf in front of some of these tall American women. How will I carry twins? Will there be enough room? What if the babies are born premature? Will the health insurance cover neonatal ICUs? What are we going to do, Varun? Will it be cheaper to give birth to the babies in India? Won't I have more help with managing things back home?"

By the time Sneha was done asking her questions, there were tears in her eyes.

Varun hadn't even thought about all these things. Would it really be better to give birth to the babies in India? But if he sent Sneha off to India, when would she be able to come back? She would not be able to travel when the babies were too young. If he sent her to India now, he would probably not be able to see her for over a year. For some reason, that did not sound like such a great idea. And what had he been saving all that money for over the years? It had been for his future and for emergencies. This certainly felt like an emergency. And with Sneha in the picture, a family had been a part of his future plan. It's just that the future had arrived a lot sooner than he expected. Looking at how miserable Sneha was, Varun decided to put up a brave front yet again.

"Don't worry," said Varun, "this is nothing! We are going to have only two babies. No matter what the expenses, I'm sure we will be fine. You know Ben? That PhD scholar in my lab? He is in the fourth year of his PhD and he and his wife pop out a baby every year. He is raising four kids on a PhD scholar's salary. I earn more money than he does. And I have some savings. We will be fine. Also, Ben told me once that there are tax deductions for babies. We have to pay less tax when we have more kids and overall it won't be so bad financially. And as far as the medical stuff is concerned, we will find out everything about the insurance and talk to the doctor and find out all our options. If pregnancy with twins ends up being difficult, we can call our parents here to help for some time."

What Varun was saying did seem to make some sense but this didn't make Sneha feel much better. She was just getting used to living in this strange country where she couldn't afford to hire maids to wash her dishes and clean her house. She was just getting used to substituting ingredients in her recipes because everything in the Indian grocery store seemed to be so expensive. She was just getting used to the idea of sharing a washing machine with complete strangers. How was she going to wash the clothes of her babies in those washing machines? How was she going to manage without a maalish wali? She still remembered how freaked out her sister had been when her baby was born a few years ago and how an expert maalish wali had been hired to give massages to the baby and the mother after the birth of the baby. The maalish wali was the only one who gave bath to her sister's tiny baby for the first few months of it's fragile life. Sneha would not have the luxury of being able to hire a maalish wali here in this strange country. On top of that, she would have to take care of two babies simultaneously. How would she manage? What would she do?

"Do you feel like having an ice cream?" Varun asked Sneha.

She shook her head.

"Let's go out for dinner tonight," he suggested.

She shook her head again.

"On the bright side," said Varun, "We'll be done in one go. If we had one baby then after a few years our parents would have pestered us to have another baby. This way, you won't have to go through the trouble of getting pregnant again."

"Getting pregnant doesn't seem to have been the trouble part," said Sneha as she wiped her tears away.

"See, if we went to Niagara Falls now," said Varun, "maybe we would have had to go there again to show it to our kids. Now what we can do is, we can plan all our travels for a few years later and kill two birds with one stone."

"You are making absolutely no sense right now," said Sneha.

"I know," said Varun.

"Let's go to Buckeye Donuts," said Sneha, "I'm craving a Devil's own."

"One sugar coated chocolate donut coming right up," said Varun as he turned the key into the ignition of the car.

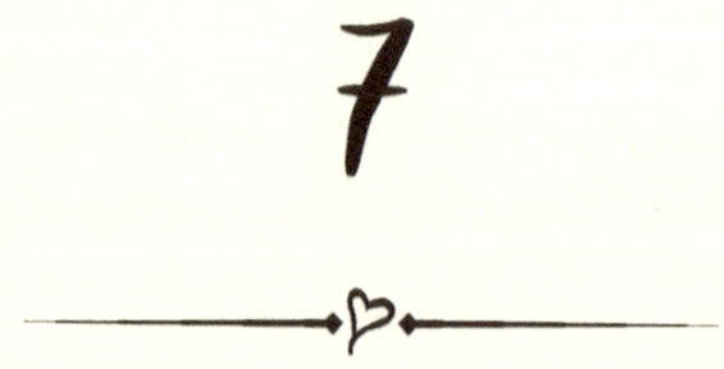

"You should be happy," Sneha's mother in-law told her, "the twins are gaining weight."

But Sneha wasn't happy. How could she be happy when she hadn't slept for more than a couple of hours at a time for the last several weeks? How could she be happy when she had aches and pains all over? How could she be happy when she hadn't even had the time to wash her hair for more than a week? How could she be happy when her husband, the person she had left her whole life for, hadn't bothered to so much as come and see her in the last two weeks? He had taken to coming home late at night and leaving early in the morning. He had all his meals outside. And even when he was at home, he slept in the living room. He didn't even enter the bedroom where Sneha was usually stuck endlessly taking care of the babies. The only adult Sneha interacted with on a daily basis was her mother-in-law.

Sneha's mother-in-law had travelled all the way from Mumbai to Columbus all alone to help Sneha and Varun with the babies.

"What will your Baba do there?" she had told Varun over the phone, "He will be another person that Sneha and I will have to take care of. Also, you yourself were saying that you have a small flat. And then Sonali and your Baba will keep each other company here."

When Sneha had conveyed this information to her mother about six months ago her mother had told her, "You should be happy. Your mother-in-law is a brave lady. She is willing to travel so far away from her home all alone at this age to help you out."

But Sneha hadn't been happy. She had wished that her own mother was the one who was making the journey. But Hetal was pregnant again and it had been decided that Sneha's mother would help Hetal out in India and Varun's mother would help Sneha out in the USA.

When the twins were born, Hetal had called Sneha. "You should be happy," Hetal had said, "even though the twins are underweight, they didn't need the neonatal ICU. You will be taking them home with you soon. This is such a blessing."

But Sneha hadn't been happy. Of course she was relieved when she found out that the babies were okay, but she was in too much pain, too sleep deprived, too uncomfortable and felt too alone to feel any positive emotion at that point.

People kept telling her how lucky she was and how happy she should be and she was getting tired of it. She was getting tired of people telling her how she was supposed to feel because she didn't feel like that at all. And she was getting tired of people telling her how to handle things because they had no idea what her situation was like anyway.

"You should put the babies to sleep at the same time and sleep when the babies are sleeping," a well meaning friend had advised her when she had called Sneha to congratulate her on the birth of her twins.

But how was Sneha supposed to ensure that? What was she supposed to do when the babies were so different from each other? They were fraternal twins and had very different weight and dietary needs. They even needed formula form two different brands. The formula that suited Tejas gave constipation to Ojas and the formula that suited Ojas gave too much gas to Tejas. It had been a nightmare figuring this whole thing out. And on top of that there was her well meaning mother-in-law making her feel inadequate.

"Why do you get such little milk?" she would say, "I used to have so much milk that I never had to feed formula to my kids. Maybe I should feed you the traditional ghee laden laddus that my mother used to feed me. But will I get all the ingredients for that here?"

How was Sneha supposed to make her mother-in-law understand that establishing a supply took time and patience, and with the underweight twins they couldn't take a chance and had to supplement the diet with formula from day one. Sneha had done everything in her power to ensure that her babies were well fed and well taken care of. She had followed all of the advice that the medical staff had given to her. She was particular about measuring out the quantities of the formula and not giving the babies any excess water so that they gained weight soon. But the problems seemed to be endless. With the jaundice to the diaper rash to the problems with latching for breast feeding; it was all quite a lot to handle. Especially when there were two very different babies to handle at the same time. On top of that was the colic. Tejas would just wail for over an hour at odd hours of the night and Sneha simply couldn't do anything about it.

"I have never seen a baby behave like this," her mother-in-law would say, "the hing always worked for my kids."

But nothing helped Tejas. He would just go on crying until he eventually fell into exhausted slumber.

"He will grow out of it eventually," is all the consolation that the medical staff could provide.

But what was Sneha supposed to do in the meanwhile?

"When will my life go back to normal?" she had asked Hetal on the phone one day.

"You are a mother now," Hetal had informed her, "you have to get used to the new normal."

But this didn't feel normal. How could this madness be normal? Where was the magical feeling of being a mother? Where was the mother-child bond? The babies hadn't even learnt how to smile yet. All Sneha got in return for her super-human efforts and her endless sleepless nights was more crying and more puke and more diaper rash. And what was more, she felt so alone in all this. Yes, her mother-in-law was also putting in a super-human effort in helping Sneha get through every single day, but Sneha was not married to her mother-in-law. These babies were as much Varun's responsibility as Sneha's. How could he just run away from all this? And how could he ignore Sneha like this when she was going through the most difficult time in her life? Sneha had just had enough of all this by now. She was fed up. So when the twins miraculously fell asleep at almost the same time that afternoon, she told her mother-in-law, "I feel like going for a walk. Please watch the kids. I'll be back soon."

"Don't worry," her mother-in-law responded, "I'll give you a ring if they wake up and I need your help."

This was the first time in weeks that Sneha had left her apartment for doing something other than going to the hospital. Summer had ended and the winds were beginning to get chilly. Sneha buttoned up her cardigan and stepped out of the apartment building. Even though she was really tired and would have loved to sleep for a couple of hours while the twins were napping, she simply had to do this. This was her chance. Her first chance in a while to have a private chat with Varun. Sneha dialed Varun's number and he picked up the phone after a few rings.

"Hello! Sneha! Is everything alright?"

"No"

"What happened?"

"I'm going crazy Varun. I need to go home."

"What are you talking about? Where are you? Aren't you at home? Where are the kids?"

"I need to go home to India. To my parents. I can't do this anymore."

There was silence on the line. So Sneha went on.

"I have some money in my account. Some savings from when I used to have a job. I can afford to buy tickets for myself and the kids. In fact even for your mother. I'll ask my parents to arrange to pick me up from Mumbai airport."

Sneha waited for some sort of response at this point too. But there was none.

"In India I can be a normal non-alien person who can get a job. I can afford a nanny for the kids. I can hire a maid to do the dishes and do the laundry. I can live like a sane person. There is nothing in this country for me."

There was still no response from Varun. It seemed like he had nothing to say. It seemed like he didn't care. Sneha was regretting agreeing to his stupid plan of giving birth to the kids in the USA. She should have flown down to India when she was in her second trimester. Life would have been a lot less lonely there. She would have had her whole extended family visit her babies by now. And even though her mother-in-law was helping out a lot, it would have been so much more comforting to have her own mother around. Sheha was tired of taking care of the babies. She needed someone to take care of her too. But since she had come to this country, she had first taken care of the apartment, then she had taken care of her husband, then she had taken care of her kids. She was exhausted. She needed Varun to be there for her. But he wasn't.

8

"Do whatever you want to do," Varun finally responded to Sneha.

He didn't have the energy to deal with this right now. He cut the call and walked back into Ross's office.

"I'm so sorry," said Varun, "I can't ignore calls from home these days."

"I understand," said Ross with a smile, "my brother has twin boys. They are identical. Him and his wife used to sometimes forget which twin was the one they had bathed. Sometimes one baby would end up getting two baths."

Varun sent a weak smile Ross's way and said, "I've sent you the final graphs and figures. Will you please upload the manuscript? I think I need to take a day off tomorrow."

"Sure thing," said Ross, "It's a Sunday. You deserve some rest. I'll upload the manuscript."

The work in the lab had been crazy the past few weeks and Varun had been working through the weekends. Varun really needed the revisions to the manuscript to be done properly if he wanted the editorial board to accept it. He had had to repeat some experiments and carry out some new experiments too. This manuscript was being considered at a high impact journal for publication. This could be a key step towards landing a respectable job as a faculty member at a good University. Varun simply couldn't let anything distract him right now. This was his dream. This was something he had worked towards for almost a decade now. Varun left Ross's office and started walking down the hallway. He had been so happy until about ten minutes ago. He had been planning to go home early and spend some time with Sneha and the kids. But with Sneha's insane behaviour over the phone he was totally pissed off. Varun had already spent so much money and put in so much effort taking care of her and the kids. The two car seats, the infinite diapers, the formula, the vitamins, the endless grocery runs, the trips to the hospital. Pregnancy and kids had come with their expenses, both monetary and time-wise. And Sneha was so busy with the kids these days that she had no time and energy to do anything else. Before the kids were born she used to take care of so many things. She would cook amazing meals, she would do the grocery, she would pay the bills, she would welcome him with a smile when he got back home from work. These days she was busy all the time and she was cranky all the time. She had totally ignored him when he had tried to explain to her the importance of this manuscript a few weeks ago.

"Just pass me the burping cloth," she had said, "I think he is done with his milk."

She hadn't even looked at him.

Varun walked down the stairwell and pushed open the door to the lobby. He stopped to look at the displays in glass cases today. He still remembered how amazed he had been the first time he saw these. He hadn't realized that the 'Newman projection' of organic molecules that he had learnt about in school was named after a faculty member who used to work at this University. An oil painting of the faculty member and a copy of his paper that was published many years ago were displayed in a glass case. There was a very old microscope kept in another display case. This was a place that valued science and meritocracy. And this was a place that had given Varun the opportunity to do research that very few labs in his home country would allow him. Varun wanted to be here. He had worked hard to be here. He deserved to be here. Varun walked to the other end of the lobby and pushed open the door. A pleasant breeze welcomed him. He took a left turn and crossed the road. He walked past the huge parking lot and then went to High Street, the main road that demarcated the end of the university area. Across the High Street he walked down to Buckeye Donuts, Sneha's favorite eatery in this area. The original idea had been to pick up some donuts for her and go home. But Varun didn't feel like it anymore.

"I'll take a Devil's own," he announced at the counter.

"For here or to go?" asked a friendly middle-aged lady from across the counter.

"For here," he said.

As Varun took a seat in the small eatery and gazed out of the huge glass window, he wondered what had gone wrong. How had his marriage come to this point? This point where his wife was running away from him. What had Varun not done for her? He had moved into a decent apartment, bought a decent car, he had cooked for her, done the dishes for her, gone shopping with her, gone on dinner dates and movies with her. He had even planned all the road-trips she wanted. And when they were both shocked by the news of the pregnancy, Varun had put on a brave face and done whatever he could to make things easier for her. He hadn't complained one bit when his mother had thrown him out of his bedroom and relegated him to the couch in the living room. He hadn't complained one bit when, after returning from a gruelling day at the lab, he was barely able to sleep at night because of the crying babies. Being married had burned a hole in his pocket and becoming a father had made the hole so much bigger. And this ungrateful woman was talking about leaving him!

Varun's reverie was broken by a phone call. It was Shreya.

"Hello," said Varun.

"Hi Varun," said Sheya, "aren't you in the lab?"

"No. I'm at Buckeye Donuts."

"Oh! Okay. How was the meeting with the boss?"

"It was fine. He said he'll submit the revised manuscript soon."

"Congratulations! And all the best. I hope it gets accepted."

"Thanks"

"Achha, listen, Anjali and I were wondering if it would be okay to drop by your place tomorrow. We wanted to meet the babies."

"Yeah, of course."

"Okay. What time would be convenient for you guys?"

"I'll let you know tomorrow morning."

∞∞∞∞

On Sunday morning, Varun was woken up by the sounds of a crying baby yet again. It was hardly 6 in the morning. He walked into the bedroom and found his mother feeding Tejas using a bottle. She smiled at Varun when he entered the room. He sat down next to her.

"Sneha had a rough night," Varun's mother told him as she looked at Sneha.

"I'm sure you had a rough night too," he retorted.

Varun's mother smiled at him and said, "She takes the first shift till 3 in the morning and then she wakes me up. But last night Ojas simply refused to fall asleep even after feeding and she couldn't sleep till 4:30 in the morning. I got some extra sleep in the process."

"Some girls from the University want to meet the babies," Varun said, "what time should I call them?"

"Any time is okay," his mother said, "the babies don't really have a schedule yet."

"Should I call them at 4 in the evening then?" suggested Varun, "It'll be tea-time."

"Yes," his mother agreed with him, "that sounds like a good idea."

Varun spent the rest of the morning preparing tea and breakfast and then he went to the grocery store to get some supplies. By the time he came back home, his mother had cooked some lunch and he got to eat a home-made lunch after many days. But throughout the day, he kept to the living room and Sneha kept to the bedroom. They barely even looked at each other.

Shreya and Anjali arrived at about 4 in the evening. The babies happened to be awake at that point and both the girls were very excited to meet the twins.

"They are so cute," said Shreya, "do you mind if I hold them?"

Sneha placed Tejas in Shreya's hands and Shreya seemed to be quite comfortable holding him.

"Varun," announced Varun's mother, "why don't you and Hema drive to the Indian grocery and get the rice and the vegetables that I had asked for? Sherya and Anjali can help me with the babies for some time."

"I can bring those on my own," said Varun.

"But you are so clueless about the fresh vegetables," his mother complained, "and I can't send Hema alone to get the huge bag of rice that we will need. So both of you have to go together. If I need help managing the babies then Shreya and Anjali can help me."

Varun looked at Sneha. She wasn't looking at him.

"Ho Aai," Varun relented.

The Indian grocery store was about 20 minutes away from where Varun and Sneha lived. They drove down to the store in silence. They barely said anything to each other while they picked up the supplies from the store. But when they got back in the car to go home, Varun simply couldn't take it anymore.

"Have you booked your tickets?" he asked Sneha, "When are you leaving?"

Sneha didn't say anything. She kept looking at the road ahead of her.

"Say something, Sneha," said Varun.

She still didn't say anything.

"What the hell Sneha?" Varun yelled at her, "How can you do this to me?"

"How can you do this to me Varun?" she yelled back, "I left my home, my family, my job, my country, my friends... I left everything for you! And now you avoid me like the plague!"

"It was your decision," said Varun, "Did anyone force you to do this? Why didn't you just marry someone in your precious Pune?"

"What was I supposed to do?" she asked him, "What was I supposed to do when I didn't like any of the guys from Pune? What was I supposed to do when the more I found out about you the less scary the idea of getting married seemed? What a fool I was! My life is scary as hell right now!"

"You think my life is a walk in the park?" responded Varun, "You have no idea the kind of pressure I have at work! What will we do if I don't get a good job? I don't want to live like a postdoc forever! You have no idea how difficult the last few weeks have been for me! The work at the lab was already killing me and then I couldn't even get a good night's sleep when I was home because the babies keep crying at odd hours of the night!"

"Don't get me started about the sleep!" Sneha snapped back at him, "I agree that you have a job and I don't so it makes sense for me to take care of things at home. But things at home are so out of control right now that I need more hands on deck! Aren't Tejas and Ojas your kids too? When was the last time you saw them?"

"What do you mean?" he retorted, "I see them every morning."

"Don't lie to me Varun," Sneha yelled back, "I saw you today after two whole weeks! You are never home! You haven't even bothered to send me a stupid message, let alone call me or talk to me. So don't go about lying to me now!"

"I see you too," said Varun, his demeanor more sad than angry now, "I see you every morning before I leave for the lab. It's just that you are sleeping at that time. It's Aai's turn to watch the kids in the morning."

"And why don't you come to the room at night when it's my turn to watch the kids?" Sneha asked him.

"What's the point trying to talk to you when you just ignore anything I say to you?"

"Oh come on Varun! I'm not the one ignoring you! You are the one who is ignoring me! I'm sick of my life right now!"

That didn't sit quite well with Varun. What more did she expect him to do?

"What can I do about that?" he said, "I had told you that the last couple of weeks were going to be hectic in the lab.

I had told you how important that manuscript is to me. I can't ignore my work. I have worked so hard for my career! How can you expect me to give that up now?"

"When did I ask you to give up your career?" she asked him.

"What do you want me to do?" he asked her, frustrated.

"I don't know," said Sneha. She was in tears by now. "I don't know what I want you to do. But I can't take this anymore. This is not what life is supposed to be like. This feels like a nightmare! Every time the kids go to sleep, I dread the time that they will wake up. I can't bear their cries any more. They are so needy and so delicate. I'm always scared I'll mess up something and ruin their lives. I don't know what I'm doing. I'm tired of taking care of the kids already. What kind of a mother am I? I think something is wrong with me Varun. Something is very wrong with me. And I don't know what to do about it."

Varun looked at Sneha. She seemed to be heartbroken and stressed out. She seemed to be so frustrated with the way things were going. Varun was frustrated too. This frustration on the home front was now to him but the frustration on the work front wasn't. When he was doing his PhD in Michigan, the last few years had been really frustrating. At that time it had seemed to him that his career was going to end. It had seemed to him that he would fail miserably at fulfilling his dream of an academic career. Many of his experiments had not been working out the way they had been expected to and his PhD supervisor was taking forever to submit the manuscripts that were written. It usually took people 5 or 6 years to finish their PhDs but it had taken Varun 7 years to finish his. But Varun had survived through those frustrating times and landed a good postdoc in Ohio. The only way Varun was going to survive the mess his life seemed to be right now was by believing that even though things weren't going exactly as planned, it would all work out in the end.

"Things will not be like this forever," Varun said to Sneha in as calm a demeanor that he could manage, "This is just a phase. The kids will grow up. I will get a good job. Then we will get a green card and you will be able to get a job if you want. Things will get better with time. I promise."

"How do you know?" asked Sneha as tears continued to stream down her cheeks, "how do you know that everything is going to be okay?"

"I don't know," said Varun, "but we have to believe. We have to believe that it is going to be okay. And we just have to get through this phase. It's just a phase in our lives. It'll be okay."

"I don't know if I can of believing in anything right now," said Sneha, "I just want to run away from here. I just want to go home. I need my mother right now. I need my family."

"Aai and I are also your family, Sneha," said Varun, "we are doing everything we can. It's just... I would have... financially it's not a good idea for us to plan a trip to India right now. We have to think about the future too."

"What future Varun?" sobbed Sneha, "I can't even imagine a future when every day is a battle. I can't even wish for the day to end. The babies don't know the difference between day and night. They keep us busy 24/7. I can't handle this."

"The work for the manuscript got finished yesterday," said Varun, "I'll help out more at home in the next few weeks. Let's take the kids for a drive in the car tonight. Remember how they both went off to sleep in their car-seats last time we came back from the hospital? I think it'll be a nice change for all of us. It'll give Aai some time to relax on her own and both of us will also get to spend some time with each other."

"Okay," said Sneha.

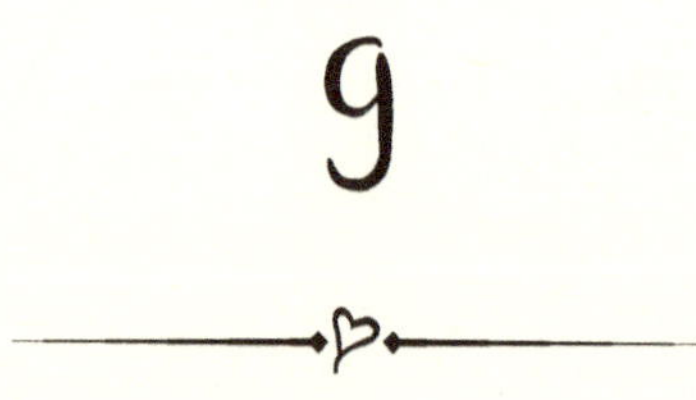

It was the summer of 2014 and Sneha was sitting on a patch of grass with her back resting against the trunk of a tree. Varun was lying down with his head in Sneha's lap and she was running her fingers through his hair.

"Have I told you lately that I love you," said Varun with his eyes closed.

"It's been a while I think," said Sneha.

"But you have to always remember that I love Tejas and Ojas more than I love you," he said, opening his eyes and smiling at her.

"I know you love me more than you love them," she declared, "I know that if Tejas and Ojas and I are drowning somewhere, you will come and save me first."

"That's only because I know that you would have grabbed them already," said Varun, "and saving you would be the fastest way of saving them."

Sneha smiled at Varun and he took her hand into his.

"Mom!" screamed Tejas, "Ojas isn't giving me the twig!"

"Dad!" screamed Ojas, "Tejas is lying!"

"I think our time is up," said Sneha. Then she yelled at her kids, "Tejas! Ojas! No fighting!"

Varun got up, dusted the back of his jeans and tugged at his T-shirt. He smiled at Sneha and said, "On the bright side, I have booked an extra room at the hotel tonight."

"Really?" asked Sneha with a coy smile as she got up and dusted off her jeans and T-shirt too.

"After all," he said, "it's the sixth anniversary of when we first met each other and we have to celebrate after the boys go off to sleep."

"Are we doing it in the bathtub tonight?" asked Sneha. And they both burst out laughing.

It had taken them over five years to get there but they were finally at Niagara Falls. The boys had enjoyed the ferry ride on the Maid of the Mist earlier that day. The ferry took them close to the waterfall and it was a fun experience for all of them. But it was Sneha who was the most excited out of the four of them.

"The American falls look so pretty," she had commented as their ferry passed by a huge waterfall. And when a rainbow emerged from the sun shining on the misty surroundings she shrieked, "Look! have you ever seen a rainbow that perfect?"

They had been given blue raincoats before boarding the ferry to protect them from the rain-like effect of being so close to the waterfall. As the ferry approached the horseshoe-shaped curtain of gushing water, the blue raincoats began to glisten even more as they got wet. Niagara Falls was so much bigger than the American falls!

"Just look at it Varun!" Sneha had screamed over the overwhelming sound of the waterfall, "can you believe how huge it is?"

Varun smiled at her and made sure he kept an eye on the kids as their mother seemed to have become a kid herself.

"I'm taking this blue raincoat home as a keepsake!" Sneha had declared after they got off the ferry and saw that everyone was giving the raincoats back to be recycled.

It was turning out to be a fun vacation for all of them and the kids were running around in an open park on the premises right now.

"Cedar Point will have to wait for a few more years," said Varun, "the boys aren't old enough for roller coasters yet."

"We have been on quite a roller coaster ourselves," said Sneha, "even if it wasn't at Cedar Point!"

The last five years had not been easy for Sneha and Varun. Giving birth to underweight twins, worrying about the baby formula not suiting them, spending one sleepless night after the other as the twins woke up alternately, worrying about introducing solid foods at the right time and potty training at the right time, worrying that the boys were growing up to be a lot more American than Indian. It had been a lot to go through. It had been quite scary at times. Of course their parents had visited from India for a few months and they had helped out. Sneha and Varun were forever thankful to have had that support system and they didn't know how they would have managed without them. When Tejas and Ojas were about a year old, Varun got a faculty position at a University in Colorado. They had moved halfway across the continent with two small babies. It had not been easy, to say the least.

On the bright side, Sneha and Varun always had each other. They didn't always agree with each other about everything and fought with each other every once in a while, but they had each other. They had each other to come back home to and make up with and cry with and laugh with. Even though moving from Ohio to Colorado had been scary and stressful, it had been exciting too. It was a new beginning in Varun's career and also in their family lives.

"I can't believe how beautiful this neighbourhood is," Sneha had commented when Varun took her to the house before finalizing the purchase.

"And there is a very good school close by," he had told her.

"I love this backyard," she had said when they opened the french windows on one side of the dining area.

"The kids will have lots of room to play and we can host barbecues in the summer," Varun had suggested.

"I can't wait to move into this house!" Sneha had declared with a smile.

The house had soon become their home, a home where their kids were growing up so fast that it was absolutely unbelievable. Apart from the hard work and stress, raising their kids had brought them innumerable moments of joy and excitement. The babies had slowly learnt the difference between night and day and Sneha gradually became less and less sleep deprived. As the babies started to grow up and learnt how to smile, she had slowly begun to feel the magic of motherhood. The first smiles, the first steps, the first words, the first doodles and the first time they came home from preschool and announced, "I love you Mom." It had all been cherished and some of it even recorded and shared. Sneha loved Varun but that love was different. In return for her love towards Varun, there was always an expectation for him to be there for her too. But with her kids Sneha had felt the kind of unconditional love that she felt for no one else in the world.

"Can you believe they will be four years old next week?" Sneha asked Varun with a smile one evening as they were enjoying some family time in the backyard.

"Time flies, doesn't it?" Varun responded.

"Only when you're lucky enough to be happy," Sneha retorted.

Sneha had found a lot of happiness in her life in this strange country. From snowfall to the fall colours in the park, she had experienced seasons in a way she had never experienced before. There were so many hiking trails and picnic spots to drive down to in and around Colorado that she didn't think they would ever be able to explore all of them. Even through the excitement of exploring the natural beauty around their new home, life had settled into a steady pace. They owned a much bigger car now and Sneha was the typical soccer mom, driving her kids to and from pre-school and soccer practice. She hadn't felt the need to get a job yet. Maybe when the kids were a bit older she would think about it. They were American citizens now and even owned a house. Sneha didn't have to worry about sharing a washing machine with strangers. She had her very own laundry room in the basement. And in another part of the basement there was a TV room that had a Bose surround sound system that Varun had always dreamed of. Varun hosted barbecues in their backyard every summer where the students from his lab got together and discussed everything from science to science fiction. Two of his graduate students had successfully passed the candidacy exams and Varun was hopeful that he would have the first PhD scholar from his lab graduate in a couple of years. It was all good. They were happy with their life now. And it had been quite a roller coaster getting here. Scary and yet so exciting!

Venuka Goyal completed her undergraduate studies from IIT Bombay and graduated as a department topper She didn't restrict herself to the library though. She was captain of the table tennis team, manager at the Entrepreneurship Cell and fulfilled other leadership roles during college. Upon graduation, she gave in to her curiosity towards science and ended up in the USA to pursue a PhD. She finished her PhD from The Ohio State University with flying colours. In her six year long stay abroad, she was bitten by the travel bug. Venuka went skydiving in Ohio, she experienced a wooden roller coaster in Kansas City and she went camping at the Yellowstone National park. After an enriching foreign exposure, Venuka returned to her roots. She has settled down in Indore, a city in central India, and teaches at a University. She is a mother to twin boys and enjoys cooking. She loves going on road trips with her family. You can find Venuka on Instagram @venuka.goyal or Facebook @venuka.goyal.author

Author's Request To The Readers

If you like what I write, please post reviews on Amazon
and Goodreads. I would really like to know what you think.